For Bess –  J.D.

For Phil –  J.S.

First published in 2003 by Macmillan Children's Books
an imprint of Pan Macmillan
20 New Wharf Road, London N1 9RR
Associated companies worldwide
www.panmacmillan.com

978-1-5098-0872-4

1 3 5 7 9 8 6 4 2

A CIP catalogue record for this book is available
from the British Library.

Printed in China

The Magic Paintbrush

Written by **Julia Donaldson**   Illustrated by **Joel Stewart**

MACMILLAN
CHILDREN'S BOOKS

"Go and catch some shrimps, Shen.
Go and catch some fish.
Go and gather oysters
To fill the empty dish."

Shen sits on the seashore.
A stick is in her hand.
She sits there drawing pictures,
Pictures in the sand.

She draws a flower, a flying fish,
She draws a boat at sea,
A hen, a hare, a dancing dog,
A weeping willow tree.

The waves roll in and wash away
The pictures in the sand.
But on a rock there sits a man.
A brush is in his hand.

He looks around. He calls to Shen.
"Come here!" he whispers. "Hush!
We don't want all the world to know
About this magic brush."

He slips the brush into her hand
And tells her to be sure
Never to paint for wealthy folk
But only for the poor.

"Did you catch some shrimps, Shen?
Did you catch some fish?
Did you gather oysters
To fill the empty dish?"

"No shrimps, no fish, no oysters!"
Shen laughs and runs inside.
She paints a pot, then stands and waits
Until the paint has dried.

The paint dries on the paper.
The painting of the pot
Is not a painting any more,
But real, and steaming hot.

"The pot is full of shrimps, Shen!
The pot is full of fish!
The pot is full of oysters
To fill the empty dish!"

The village people hear the news.
Into the house they crush.
The young and old all want to see
Shen and her magic brush.

She paints a melon for a boy,
A ladder for a man,
A basket for a woman,
And for a girl, a fan.

And soon the news spreads far and wide
And people stand in queues
For blankets, boats and buffaloes,
For hats and coats and shoes.

The news spreads over fields of rice
And over desert sands,
Until at last, inside Shen's house
The powerful Emperor stands.

"I order you to paint a tree
And make it very big.
Instead of leaves, paint golden coins,
A hundred on each twig."

Shen shakes her head. "Your Majesty,
I promised to be sure
Never to paint for wealthy folk
But only for the poor."

The Emperor scowls and stamps his foot.
He bellows to his men,
"Seize the magic paintbrush
And seize the girl called Shen."

Now Shen sits in a prison
Upon a cold stone floor.
She waits there till the Emperor
Opens the prison door.

He holds the magic paintbrush.
He orders, "Paint that tree!
Paint me my tree of golden coins
And then you shall go free."

Shen takes the brush, and bowing low
Says, "Gracious Majesty,
Come back here in the morning
And you shall have your tree."

That night the Emperor lies in bed
And dreams about his tree,
While Shen is busy painting
A horse and then a key.

The key turns in the prison door
And Shen stands free outside.
She climbs on to the horse's back
And swiftly starts to ride.

"Where are my coins?" the Emperor shouts.
"Where is my golden tree?
Where is the magic brush?" he cries.
"Who let the girl go free?"

He climbs on to his fastest horse
And rides with all his men.
Over the fields and desert sands
They gallop after Shen.

"It's Shen! It's Shen! She's back again!"
The neighbours gather round.
But Shen is painting silently
While distant hoofbeats sound.

She paints a mighty river.
A river deep and wide.
The Emperor and all his men
Stop on the other side.

The Emperor scowls and stamps his foot.
He shakes his fist at Shen.
  "I'll swim across your river,
    And so will all my men."

But Shen is busy painting.
A beast with scales and claws.
Its scarlet wings are open
And flames curl from its jaws.

"My dragon needs a tail," says Shen,
"And then it will be real.
Yes, then it will be roaring
And ready for a meal.

"Now shall I paint that tail?" she asks.
"Or would you rather go?"
She dips her brush into the pot.
The Emperor cries out, "No!"

He turns his horse and rides away.
Away ride all his men.
Shen takes the magic paintbrush
And starts to paint again.

She paints a mound of golden rice
And cakes like little moons,
And drums and flutes, till all the streets
Ring out with merry tunes.

The sun goes down. The moon comes out
And shines as bright as day
While Shen and all the villagers
Dance the night away.